Jill Dow trained at the Royal College of Art, and since graduating has worked as a freelance illustrator specializing in natural history. She illustrated the highly successful series *Bellamy's Changing World*, but the *Windy Edge Farm* stories are the first books she has both written and illustrated.

Jill Dow lives in Robertsbridge, East Sussex.

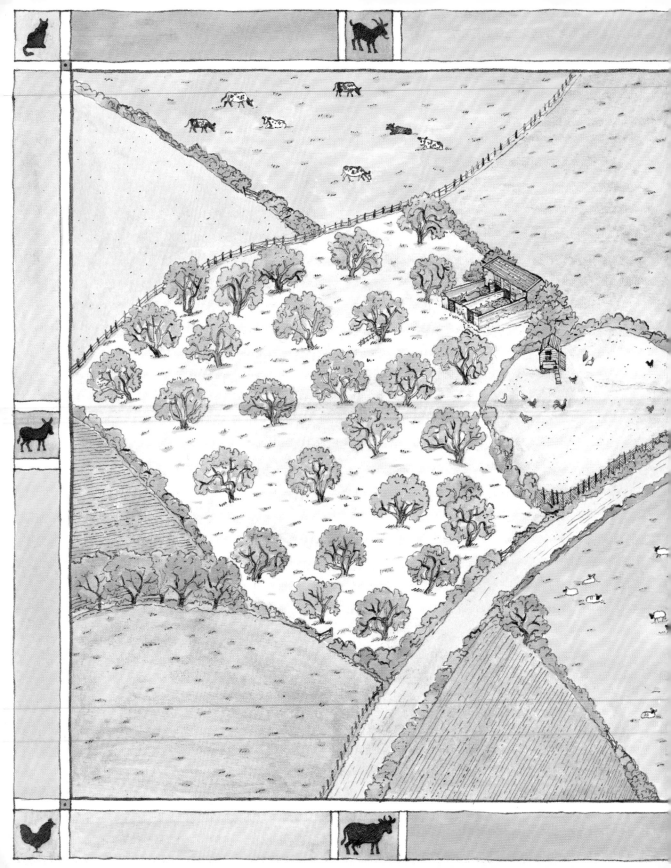

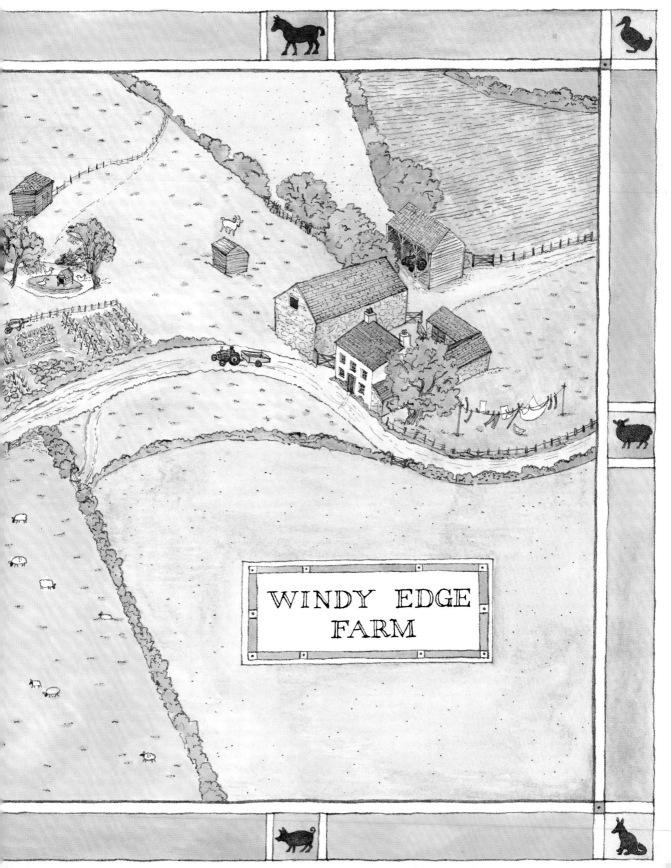

WINDY EDGE
FARM

*For Erin*

Text and illustrations copyright © Jill Dow 1990

First published in Great Britain in 1990 by
Frances Lincoln Limited, Apollo Works
5 Charlton Kings Road, London NW5 2SB

British Library Cataloguing in Publication Data
Dow, Jill
Webster's walk.
I. Title   II. Series
823'.914 [J]

ISBN 0-7112-0613-9 hardback
ISBN 0-7112-0614-7 paperback

Set in Century Schoolbook by Goodfellow & Egan
Printed and bound in Hong Kong

First Frances Lincoln Edition: April 1990

3   5   7   9   8   6   4

Design and art direction Debbie MacKinnon

WINDY EDGE FARM

# WEBSTER'S WALK

## Jill Dow

FRANCES LINCOLN

In the middle of summer Windy Edge Farm was a dry and dusty place. It had not rained for weeks and weeks, and all the animals felt hot and grumpy.

The hens used the rhubarb plant as if its leaves were parasols, and the pigs kicked over their water trough and rolled in the mud to cool their baking skins.

Most upset of all were the ducks. The scorching sun had dried up all the water in their pond.

Now the only water they had was in a tub that Angus filled up every day.

One morning Angus told the ducks he was going
to have a swim in the river. "Why don't you
come too?" he said, sloshing water into their tub.

But only Webster heard him – the others were
all too busy squabbling over whose turn it was to
have a splash in the shallow water.

All day Webster wondered about
the river. What was it? Where was it?
If Angus was going there to swim,
it must be a very watery place.
Webster began to plan.

Early next morning, Webster hopped on to the
rim of the tub and stood up tall. "Today," he
quacked, "I'm going to find the river. Who's
coming with me?"

"I'll come," said Wilma, who followed Webster
everywhere.

"And me!" quacked Winnie, who never let
Wilma out of her sight.

One by one all the ducks joined the line.

Webster led them past the pigsty . . .

and through the orchard, where they found
the goats.

"Excuse me," said Webster politely,
"do you know the way to the river, please?"

But Clover and Hazel didn't bother to reply.
They were too busy trying to pull the washing
off the line.

In the cornfield they came across a very scruffy gentleman.

"Do you know the way to the river, please?" Webster asked him.

But the man stayed silent, and kept on pointing in two different directions.

Now Webster was more confused than ever, but he waddled on, with all the other ducks behind him.

But they *were* on the right road after all! At last they reached a place where lots of water was flowing along between shady banks.

Webster quacked with relief as he waddled down the bank and dipped his hot, aching feet in the water. The others plunged in after him and they all set off across the river.

It was very different from their old pond, where the water had been warm and murky. Here it was cool, and so clear that they could see right down to the bottom.

Most surprising of all, *this* water kept on moving. The ducks discovered that they didn't need to paddle with their feet, because the river carried them along. But when they turned round and tried to swim back again it was much more difficult!

They dipped their heads in the cool water and turned right upside-down to have a better look. There were all sorts of tasty things to eat amongst the waterweeds, and the ducks realised just how hungry they were.

As they drifted downstream, they met some of
the wild birds that lived beside the river – the
beautiful swans, the silent heron, the shy
moorhen and the brilliant kingfisher.

They even met some birds who looked just
like they did, except their feathers were green
and brown and grey instead of white. How lucky
these wild ducks were, thought Webster, to have
the river as their home.

The ducks were so busy enjoying themselves that they didn't notice the huge dark clouds gathering in the sky. The reed warblers stopped chattering in the rushes, and a strange silence fell over the river. Suddenly a brilliant flash lit up the sky, and thunder began to crack and roar.

The ducks were scared, and even Webster wished that he was back in the farmyard. They huddled together under the bridge, and watched in silence as huge, heavy drops of rain splashed faster and faster on to the river, spreading great ripples over the surface.

In a while the storm stopped as suddenly as it had begun, and the sun crept out from behind the clouds. But the river no longer seemed such a friendly place, and the ducks set off wearily for home.

Just then, Mrs Finlay and Angus came driving along. They saw the line of ducks straggling up the road, and managed to stop just in time.

"*There* you are!" cried Angus, jumping out. "We wondered where you'd got to." And he helped the ducks into the back of the pick-up.

The dogs teased them as they bumped and rattled along, but the ducks didn't care. They would soon be home at Windy Edge Farm!

And when they arrived, they found that the rain had filled up their pond again! With quacks of delight they waddled down the bank and plopped into the water.

Webster thought of the river, with its cool water and shady banks. But this old pond was still his favourite place. Round and round he swam, with all the other ducks behind, until the sun went down.

– The End –